Dear Parent:

Congratulations! Your child is taking the first steps on an exciting journey. The destination? Independent reading!

STEP INTO READING® will help your child get there. The program offers five steps to reading success. Each step includes fun stories and colorful art. There are also Step into Reading Sticker Books, Step into Reading Math Readers, Step into Reading Write-In Readers, Step into Reading Phonics Readers, and Step into Reading Phonics First Steps! Boxed Sets—a complete literacy program with something for every child.

Learning to Read, Step by Step!

Ready to Read   Preschool–Kindergarten
• big type and easy words • rhyme and rhythm • picture clues
For children who know the alphabet and are eager to begin reading.

Reading with Help   Preschool–Grade 1
• basic vocabulary • short sentences • simple stories
For children who recognize familiar words and sound out new words with help.

Reading on Your Own   Grades 1–3
• engaging characters • easy-to-follow plots • popular topics
For children who are ready to read on their own.

Reading Paragraphs   Grades 2–3
• challenging vocabulary • short paragraphs • exciting stories
For newly independent readers who read simple sentences with confidence.

Ready for Chapters   Grades 2–4
• chapters • longer paragraphs • full-color art
For children who want to take the plunge into chapter books but still like colorful pictures.

STEP INTO READING® is designed to give every child a successful reading experience. The grade levels are only guides. Children can progress through the steps at their own speed, developing confidence in their reading, no matter what their grade.

Remember, a lifetime love of reading starts with a single step!

For Anthony
—A.J.

www.stepintoreading.com

Educators and librarians, for a variety of teaching tools, visit us at www.randomhouse.com/teachers

Library of Congress Cataloging-in-Publication Data
Jordan, Apple.
Bug stew! / by Apple Jordan.
    p. cm. — (Step into reading. A step 1 Book)
SUMMARY: An easy-to-read, rhyming tale of Timon, Pumbaa, and Simba, who spend a day searching for and eating all sorts of tasty bugs.
ISBN 0-7364-2168-8— ISBN 0-7364-8025-0 (lib. bdg.)
[1. Insects—Fiction. 2. Lions—Fiction. 3. Warthog—Fiction. 4. Meerkat—Fiction. 5. Africa—Fiction. 6. Stories in rhyme.]   I. Title. II. Series: Step into reading.
Step 1 book. PZ8.3.J7645Bu 2003 [E]—dc21   2002154061

Printed in the United States of America   10   9

DISNEY'S
THE
LION KING

Bug Stew!

by Apple Jordan
illustrated by Robbin Cuddy

Random House 🏠 New York

Timon and Pumbaa
love bugs.
Yum!

Simba learns to
like them, too.

Time to hunt
for more bugs!

The friends go
find a few.

They look under rocks.
They look up in trees.

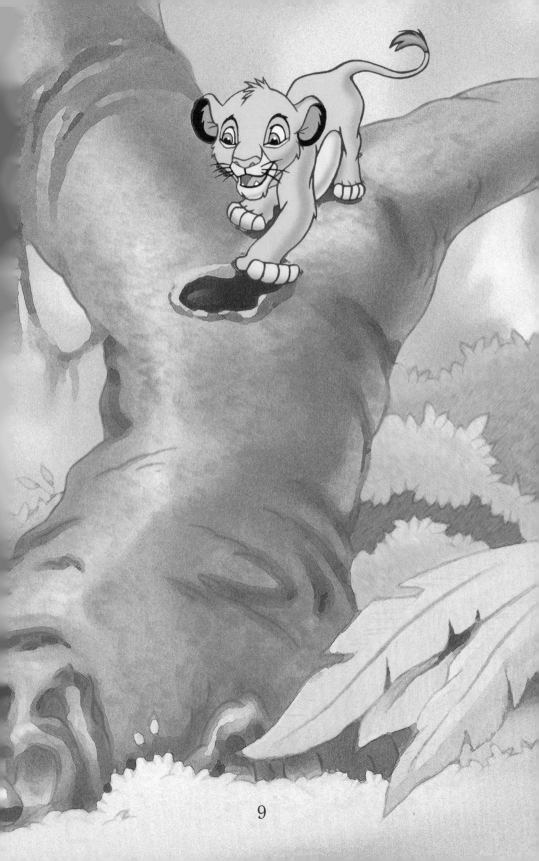

They find fat flies.

They find bumblebees.

They look inside logs
for slimy slugs.

They look and they look
for all types of bugs.

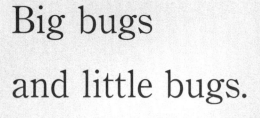

Big bugs
and little bugs.

Fuzzy, furry,
wiggly bugs.

Crunchy bugs,
sticky bugs.
Chewy, gooey,
icky bugs.

Bugs that can sting.

Bugs that hop high.

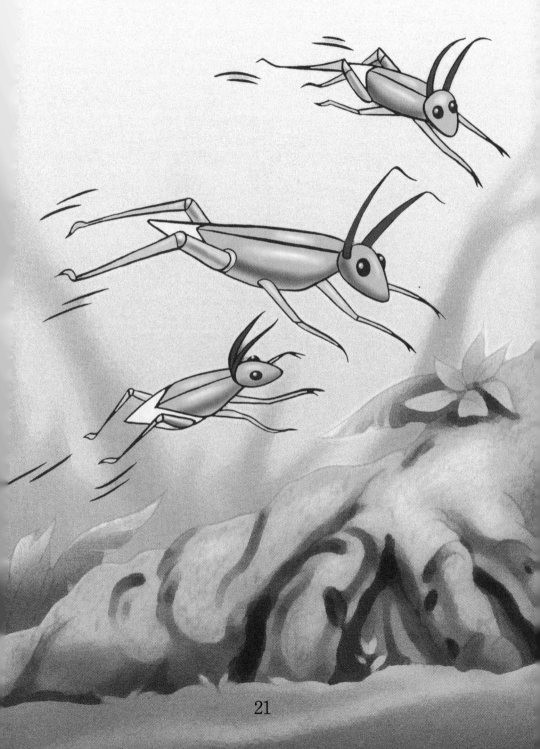

Bugs with big wings.

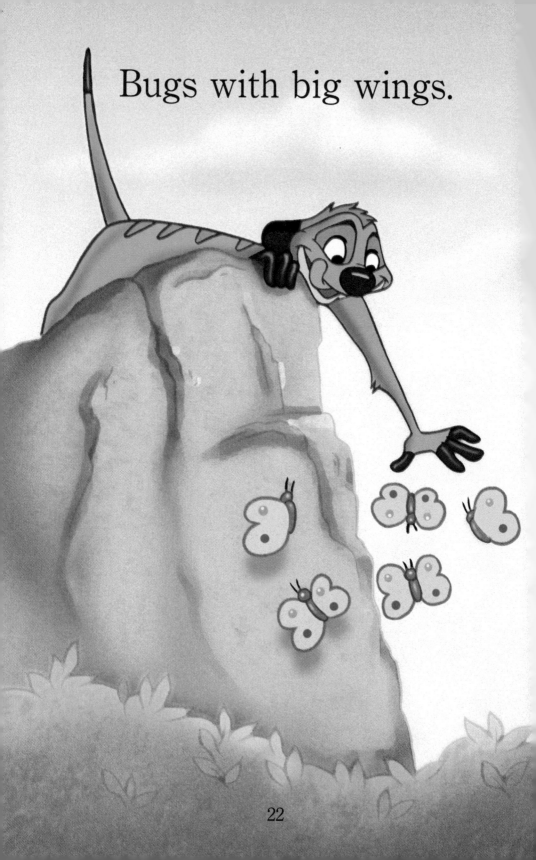

Bugs that can fly.

Bugs that run fast.

Bugs that crawl slow.

Bugs that can swim.

Bugs that can glow.

They have
buckets of bugs.
Now what will they do?

Mix them all up
and make a bug stew!